FEAR OF BARBARIANS

FEAR OF BARBARIANS

Petar Andonovski

Translated by
Christina E. Kramer

PARTHIAN

CYNGOR LLYFRAU CYMRU
BOOKS COUNCIL of WALES

Creative
Europe

Co-funded by the Creative Europe Programme of
the European Union

Petar Andonovski was born in 1987, in Kumanovo, North Macedonia. He studied at the University of Cyril and Methodius in Skopje. His novels include *Eyes the Color of Shoes*, *The Body One Must Live In*, which received the Macedonian novel of the year award. The *Fear of Barbarians* was published in 2018 and won the European Prize for Literature. He has also published a collection of poetry, *Mental Space*. His latest novel is *Summer Without You* (2020).

Christina E. Kramer is a Professor Emerita in the Department of Slavic languages and Literatures at the University of Toronto, Canada. In addition to her numerous articles relating to Balkan linguistics and a Macedonian grammar (University of Wisconsin Press), she is also a literary translator. Her translations include *A Spare Life* by Lidija Dimkovska (Two Lines Press) *Freud's Sister* by Goce Smilevski (Penguin Books) and three novels by Luan Starova *My Father's Books*, *The Time of the Goats* (University of Wisconsin Press, 2012), and *The Path of the Eels* (Autumn Hill Books). Her translations also appear in numerous journals including *Asymptote*, *Chicago Review*, *Two Line Online*, *M-Dash*, *Tin House*, *a Words without Borders*, *World Literature Today* and others.

For my mother, and for Liljana Dirjan,
and Elizabeta Mukaetova Ladinska

Parthian, Cardigan SA43 1ED
www.parthianbooks.com
© Petar Andonovski 2018
First published as СТРАВ ОД ВАРВАРИ by Ili-Ili, Skopje, 2018
Translated by Christina E. Kramer copyright 2021
ISBN print: 978-1-91364-019-4
ISBN ebook: 978-1-913640-36-1
Editor: Jennifer Barclay
Cover Design: Syncopated Pandemonium
Typeset by Elaine Sharples
Printed by 4edge Ltd, UK
Published with the financial support of the Welsh Books Council and
Co-funded by the Creative Europe Programme of the European Union
British Library Cataloguing in Publication Data
A cataloguing record for this book is available from the British Library.

Art thou not it which hath dried the sea, the waters of the great deep;
that hath made the depths of the sea a way
for the ransomed to pass over?

Isaiah 51:10

POSTCARD: OKSANA

I don't know how much time has passed since our last meeting. From today's distance it seems like it was in another lifetime. Once you were gone, I thought I would never leave Ukraine, I would stay in Donetsk my whole life and wait for your return. But I left Donetsk a long time ago, and a short time ago I even left Ukraine. Just think, I now live on an island, wherever I look I see the sea, though for now I see it only through the windows of our house. They are large and there's a good view, so no matter what room I enter, I see the sea before me. It's huge! Just as we imagined it. The house is also like the one in the postcard your father brought you, white, two-story, the window frames are blue, the shutters are also blue, and in front of the door there's a lemon tree. Do you remember when I was sick and you came to visit me, outside it was snowing, really snowing a lot, and you brought me two lemons. I told you I was cold, and you stroked my forehead and told me not to worry, that one day we would go to an island in Greece where we would always be warm, and we wouldn't have just two lemons, but a whole orchard of lemons, we would live in a house like the one in the postcard your father brought you. After so many years, I really did move to an island, I live in a house like the one in the postcard your father brought you, and I have a lemon tree, but I live with Evgenii and Igor, not with you. You don't even know who Evgenii is.

It was afternoon when Evgenii and I met in a lecture hall at the university. It was afternoon when the two of us—both just graduated—were called to the dean's office and told that since we were the best students, we were going to be employed at the nuclear power station in Chernobyl. It was afternoon when we learned that there had been a meltdown in the fourth reactor of the Lenin nuclear power station.

It was afternoon when the fisherman threw the rope to the people gathered, and we stepped onto the island for the first time.

Evgenii and I had been living together the past few years in Kiev. Everything we had was left behind in Pripyat. One morning, Evgenii happened to run into Igor, our colleague at the power plant, who we thought had died in the explosion. He told Evgenii that he'd moved to Crete after the accident and was living there in a village near Psiloritis. No one lives in the village except a few old people and some cats. He survives by helping out the old people and shepherds from the surrounding villages, and in return they give him food and a bit of money. He managed to get cured of radiation there. All these years Evgenii has been constantly sick, he's constantly undergoing various tests. As Igor was leaving, he told Evgenii that he was home because his father was in the hospital, but he was going back in a few weeks, this time to an island near Crete. To Gavdos.

BOAT OF FEAR: PENELOPE

If you hadn't fled the convent that night, we would now most likely be somewhere in Spain or Portugal. That afternoon when the fisherman tied the rope to the harbour dock, I knew I would always remain here. The day I stepped foot on Gavdos, I promised myself I would never think of you again. And I didn't for ten whole years, until today, when Mihalis returned home upset. I saw fear in his face for the first time. He said that since early morning, people had been gathering in the taverna to greet the doctor. While they drank raki, the priest asked the doctor what was new over there, gesturing across the sea. He told them the Berlin Wall had fallen, and all of Europe was in a state of anticipation. Everyone was silent. It wasn't clear to anyone how some wall in Europe could have any significance.

Here people live for years forgotten, history persistently passes them by, even leprosy and hunger had passed them by, and just when they thought it would pass them by again, Spiros flew into the taverna and, according to Mihalis, began shouting at full volume: "They've arrived! There they are, they're pulling into the harbour!" And without asking who they were, everybody set off towards the harbour of Karave. There, in the middle of the calm sea, drawing closer and closer, there, in the shape of a boat, was fear.

Three people stepped out of the boat, two men and a woman. The woman had short-cropped hair and looked more like a man than a woman. The fisherman who brought them said they had come to get cured on the island. He said they were Russians.

Then my blood froze! Not from fear! But from the thought of

you! I saw you standing there; you have that smile on your face that Sister Theoktisti called devilish. You laugh at them ironically while looking at the fear in their eyes. You who said you weren't afraid of anything, not even of death.

Do you remember when those two Americans came to the convent and said they were journalists and wanted to photograph the girls who lived there, but Sister Erotea hopped about nervously on one foot and kept repeating, while glancing at the windows of Sister Theoktisti's study, that Sister Superior Theoktisti wasn't there; she was visiting the monastery in Arkadi. And after a long discussion with the Americans, you dragged me by the arm and told them we would pose. We stood and posed. The whole time I looked shamefully at my shoes covered in dust while you shamelessly made faces at the camera. Sister Erotea stood to the side and threatened you the whole time, saying she would tell Sister Theoktisti about you, but to me she merely said that I was shaming myself by following your example, you were half a foreigner so such behaviour could be expected of you, but not me. I never told you that I was also a little afraid of them, and at the same time I was afraid of disappointing you because you kept saying that I was different, that I wasn't like the other girls.

DREAM: OKSANA

I dreamt I was looking for a post office so I could send you a postcard. I am going from one lane to another, you know, those alleyways like the ones we have only here in the Mediterranean, narrow, lined with stone houses; whenever I come to the end of the street, in front of me there is the sea, huge, so huge you can't tell where it ends and the sky begins. At one moment, I understand that I am not on Gavdos, this is some other island. I try to remember how I got there, and while I hopelessly attempt to recall at least one detail that would lead me to the place I came from, I remember the postcard and that my address might be on it—but not only is nothing written there, the postcard is old and faded, its image barely recognisable, there's an old dilapidated house, its white paint barely discernible, and the blue of its window frames and shutters so imperceptible that from a distance there appear to be no windows. The lemon tree is old and withered, with a single yellow lemon hanging from it, a reminder that this tree once bore fruit, an abundance of fruit.

I was awakened from my dream by Evgenii's loud coughing. He was holding a bloodied handkerchief in his hand. Frightened by my dream and by Evgenii's cough, I went to look for Igor, but he wasn't in the house. Evgenii wanted me to bring him some water. The jug in the kitchen was empty, so I had to go outside to draw water from the well. That was my first time leaving the house in three days. Ever since we arrived, Igor had been saying it would be best if I didn't go out of the house for a while until the islanders got used to us. Every morning he and Evgenii would go out at dawn, walk along the seashore to catch fish, and they would bring the fish back for me to cook. This was the first morning that Evgenii didn't go with him.

Outside, a warm breeze was blowing. The smell of the salt stirred my nostrils – if I could just go down to the sea, sit on a craggy rock and look across the sea's endless expanse. When we arrived on Crete, Igor took us to Agia Roumeli and told us we would find a fisherman there who would take us across to Gavdos. Boats rarely come here. We stayed about a month in Agia Roumeli – not a single fisherman was willing to take on the job of transporting us as far as Gavdos, we would have to wait until spring, but Igor kept offering one of them more and more money until they somehow came to an agreement.

I didn't know exactly where the well was, I circled the house a few times but didn't find anything. A hundred or so metres away there's another house; this is a small village, there are only about three houses. Igor told me there is another house on the way out of the village, the part that people call the women's village on account of the two old women who live there. When I got to the other house, I saw a woman drawing water from a well. When she saw me, the bucket fell from her hands. The water poured over her feet. She stood there and looked at me, she had blue eyes like the sea, she didn't look at me with fear but with disbelief, I wanted to say something to her but I couldn't, my voice had suddenly vanished. I opened my mouth, but it was useless, nothing came out. I don't know how long we stood like this: she with her frozen look, I with my open mouth from which nothing emerged. A young girl came out of the house. She looked at us with curiosity, and when she reached the woman, she took her by the hand and they went into the house. I continued standing there with my mouth open and looked at the door they had entered, the woman then glanced out the window, and when she saw that I was still standing there, she turned away. I don't know how long I stood there. When I glanced towards our house, I saw Igor observing me, his look full of reproach.

THE COLOUR OF SNOW: PENELOPE

All night I tried to recall your voice. But what came to me again and again was the image of the first day you arrived at the convent. You were sitting there on a bench, looking at us, smirking. You weren't like us, we were all the same, our hair was braided, we all wore black dresses with white collars that Sister Dionysia had sewn for us, but you had long blond hair and wore a red dress. None of us had ever seen a colourful dress until that moment; we always wore black except for Easter and for the Dormition of the Virgin Mary, when we wore white dresses. Your grandmother, who brought you to the convent, was standing there with Sister Theoktisti talking about something when she suddenly began to cry and Sister Theoktisti comforted her; later, Olympia told us that your mother had run off. After she abandoned your father, he and your grandmother decided to bring you to the convent because they were afraid you might also run off.

All week you didn't say a word to anyone, until the day I was sitting on the terrace, drawing the Virgin. I wanted her to have a white dress, white like the snow on Psiloritis. I kept trying to get the colour right, and you came up to me, took the brush from my hand, mixed a few colours and said there, that's the colour; I just sat there and looked at you in bewilderment. I never found out how you knew I wanted the Virgin's dress to be white like the snow on Psiloritis. Later, at lunch, you sat beside me and told me that you knew right from the beginning as soon as you saw me that I wasn't like the other girls. When Olympia saw you talking to me, she came over and asked you if you had finally broken

8

your vow of silence and she began to laugh; you gave her a look full of irony, and told her that you would take your vows before she did. Everyone in the convent knew that Sister Theoktisti didn't like Olympia, and that she had been trying a long time to marry her off, but simply couldn't find a man to take her. When Olympia turned twenty-five, she said she wanted to take her vows, but Sister Theoktisti kept dissuading her, hoping that someone would come along who would want her for his wife. From that day on Sister Theoktisti no long paid any attention to you, she constantly avoided you, but once, while I was helping her with lunch, she told me to be careful around you, that you were an absolute devil.

But I wanted more and more to be near you, I was ready to do anything so as not to disappoint you. That day you sat next to me during lunch and asked whether I was planning to enrol in an art academy, I told you I was planning to, even though I had no plans for the future, I knew nothing about life, I wanted to stay in the convent even after I turned sixteen, to take care of the girls and, by painting icons, to help the convent financially. Sister Theoktisti slowly prepared me for life in the convent. She tried every way she could to keep the girls who had some talent in the convent, and for those who didn't, she found wealthy husbands who would then help her.

In the convent I was the only one who had no one. The other girls had been brought by their families when they reached puberty. Not only did nuns teach us to read and write, they also taught us how to embroider and knit, they taught us about fidelity and love, and then, when their wards turned sixteen, if their families hadn't found an opportunity to marry them, Sister Theoktisti found it for them. When one of the wards was of marriageable age, we were taken to the market in Timbaki on a

Friday, or to the market in Mires on Saturday. Out in front rode Sister Theoktisti mounted on a donkey, behind her went Sister Dionysia with the marriageable girl, and behind them all the rest of us passed by the tavernas where men were sitting; we all looked at the ground, not daring to look at them, the only one who dared to look was the girl who was to be married. Once, Sister Erotea told me they had brought Olympia out for nearly an entire year, but no one ever came forward, and finally her time had passed.

I never told you how I came to the convent, although I think you knew and never asked me. When I was two years old, my mother died of tuberculosis, leaving behind my father and me. He was a fisherman and was at sea more than on land, there was no one to look after me, so he took me to the convent when I was four years old. Every weekend he would come to fetch me, take me to our house in Kokkinos Pirgos and then return me to the convent. On my seventh birthday he came to the convent and brought me a doll – it was my first and only doll – that he had bought at a shop in Athens. He said that he would go out fishing one more week, and then he'd come for me and would never leave me again, he told me he had collected enough money to open a small taverna, and I would go to school, and then I'd help him. That was the longest week of my life. I thought it would never end. When the day finally came, Sister Dionysia got me ready to leave. I stood impatiently on the convent stairs and waited for him to come, my left hand holding tightly to the doll he had brought me. But he didn't come. I waited the next day, and the one after that and the following weeks and months, he didn't come. When I turned fourteen, the day before you came to the convent, Sister Theoktisti told me that she and I would go for a walk through the olive groves behind the convent. While we were walking, she told me that I needed to know the truth about why my father never came that day. I don't know whether I wanted to hear the truth, I was more afraid of it than the fact that he hadn't come. She told me that the night he came to visit me in the convent, he had gone out in a boat; there was a terrible storm that night and it was too much for the boat; it was an old boat and not even his; he had borrowed it. His body was never found, but several weeks after the accident some fisherman found the plank on which the name of the boat was written, *Elpida*. That was the boat's name: *Hope*.

WOMEN IMPRISONED ON THE ISLANDS: OKSANA

This morning Igor went off to see the doctor about coming to examine Evgenii. Even though Igor said the doctor had promised yesterday evening he would come, this morning he refused, saying he couldn't because he'd have problems later on with the islanders. Evgenii ran a temperature all night; he was coughing constantly and spitting up blood. Igor said he'd try once more to convince him. The doctor is from Crete; he comes to Gavdos on the last boat in the autumn and goes back on the first in the spring. No one apparently wants to accept work on Gavdos, there isn't even a clinic here, and he's not even a real doctor, they say that he abandoned his medical studies in his fourth year.

After Igor went out to catch fish for lunch and Evgenii had finally fallen asleep, I went out into the courtyard again. Outside a warm wind was blowing even though it was December. I went over to the other house, but no one was there. No one appeared, not even the woman who had looked at me in disbelief. I returned home and lay down beside Evgenii. Later I dreamt that it was snowing outside, lots of snow, we are lying in your father's study, there are maps of islands strewn about everywhere, you peel an orange and you give me a piece, and suddenly the whole room begins to smell of oranges, you pull a map from the pile and you point to an island and you say that only women live on this island, their husbands are sailors and whoever leaves never returns, in the summer fishermen come to the island and spend their nights with the women, but in the winters when the rain doesn't stop for days, the women remain closeted in their stone houses and write poetry. They all write the same verses. There is no reason for me not to believe you, your father is a cartographer, who loves most of all to draw maps of islands; he knows everything about them.

When I awoke, it had already grown dark outside. Evgenii was sitting up and looking at me; he told me that I had been laughing in my sleep the whole time. We stayed a bit longer in bed; I don't remember when we last sat together like this. I wanted to tell him that ever since we came to Gavdos I have been thinking of you all the time, but I've never mentioned you, I don't know whether I thought of you a single time all these years. Since the day you left, I promised myself I would forget you completely, that seemed easiest, but it was only after I left Donetsk and went to study in Kiev that I stopped remembering you. Evgenii saw that I was lost in thought, and he said he would let me lie there for a bit while he got up and moved about the room a little, but he couldn't stand up, he had absolutely no strength even though he seemed better. I told him not to hurry, I would go see what was happening with Igor. When I went down to the kitchen, I saw that Igor had not come back at all. I went outside to see whether he was in the yard, but he wasn't there either. I didn't know what to do. I stood for a while in the yard then I noticed that not far away from our house someone was standing there looking at me. It was the woman with the blue eyes. I said 'good evening' to her quietly, in Russian, she had that same look, full of disbelief, I said 'good evening' to her again, this time in Greek, greetings were the only thing I knew, it was then I noticed she had an armful of wood, and when I took a step closer to her, she threw down the wood and ran towards her house. As I watched her run, I felt someone's breath behind me, when I turned I saw Igor, he threw me a curt look and, uttering not a word to me, turned and headed towards the house.

When I went in, he was standing there facing the table. Without looking at me, he said, 'This is it for today, I barely managed to catch one fish.' I didn't know what to say, I took the fish and immediately began cleaning it. He went off to his room and, without turning towards me, said, 'Make soup with it, give the fish to Evgenii, he needs to get stronger.'

I brought Evgenii a plate of food. When I attempted to put the spoon in his mouth, he pushed my hand away and said that even though he was sick, he wasn't a cripple and could still feed himself. Then he asked me to leave him alone in the room. When I went downstairs, Igor was sitting at the table, he had set out plates and spoons, we ate in silence. After our dinner he apologized for his stupid behaviour, he hadn't wanted to insult me, but he was worried that something could happen to me. I said nothing, I gathered up the plates and went to the kitchen. A short time later he followed me in and told me he had a small present for me. From the inside pocket of his coat he pulled out a stone – turquoise, egg-shaped. 'I took it from the sea for you,' he said. I took the stone gently as if it were made of the thinnest glass and could easily break. Igor told me he was going to change his clothes. I brought the stone to my mouth and licked it with the tip of my tongue. It was salty. I licked it again. Suddenly I began licking it wildly until I had licked off all the salt. Then I lay on the kitchen floor and began to cry. I sobbed loudly. When I saw Igor standing in the doorway looking at me I stood up, wiped away my tears and told him to tell me how he had spent the day, what colour the sea was, whether there were waves or it was calm, to tell me everything, and also to tell me how he found the stone, why this stone and not some other, I wanted to know everything. Igor took me by the hand and led me to the table, sat down opposite me, he was silent for a while and watched a spider descending from the ceiling towards the window, then he began:

'Since I caught only a single fish yesterday down by Sarakiniko beach, I decided to do something different today. While I was returning from the doctor, I remembered that the fisherman who had brought me here told me there was a lighthouse on the island, and if the sea is choppy you can catch the most fish there. The fisherman told me that the lighthouse keeper and his crazy wife live just beside the lighthouse; he told me that if I went there, I'd likely see her, she's always standing on the rocks looking out to sea, she has long hair almost down to her feet, and if I saw her, it would be best not to go near her because she could be aggressive. When I got to the lighthouse, I went down to the sea along the goat path. When I reached the shore, I saw to the right of me a woman standing on a rock looking out to the sea. But she didn't resemble at all the fisherman's description. Her hair came down to her shoulders, she was behaving normally, she wore a grey dress, a bit faded but it looked clean, she didn't give any sign at all of being crazy. I stood there awhile and looked at her, she didn't glance at me even once, I think she was looking towards Crete. That's the best place to see Crete, although it looks like a splotch between the sky and the sea. When I stepped closer to the sea, she turned and ran towards me. I stood there looking at her in confusion. When she was a step away from me, she looked into my eyes. Her look was wild, but not crazy. Her face was tender, she acted exhausted as if she had no strength for anything, least of all to harm anyone. After a long and uncomfortable silence, she said to me, "Show me your palm." It sounded more like a command than a request. I cautiously raised my hand and showed it to her. Her own palm was tender, I felt all at once that I could trust her. She looked at it awhile thoughtfully, as if she were reading my fate. Then she said to me, "I see water... a lot of water... and a boat... far away... very far... it is barely visible..." With her finger, she pointed to the end of my lifeline.

Then she let go of my hand, and taking fright, she began to run from me along the goat path, and while she was running, she turned several times to see whether I was following her. After she disappeared somewhere near the lighthouse, I sat on the rock where she had been standing and looked at the sea, I thought about that woman for hours. When it began to grow dark, I remembered I hadn't caught a single fish. That's why I returned so late.'

'And the stone?' I asked quietly. He looked at me as if he didn't know what I was talking about, then he said, 'I found the stone there, on the rock, I think she was holding it in her hand and when she ran towards me, she left it.'

I began to squeeze the stone tightly, then I told him I was tired and that I was going to lie down, but all I wanted was for the next evening to come quickly and for him to tell me new tales.

TEMPTATION: PENELOPE

Mihalis returned late at night. Irini was asleep in the bed beside us. When Mihalis came in, I pretended to be asleep. That woman, the Russian one, came again today, she stood there looking at our house. Mihalis lay down beside me and began gently touching my breasts, he drew close to my ear and said, 'Wake up,' his breath smelled of raki and his body of sheep, I thought I would vomit, I shut my eyes as tight as possible, but again he said, 'Wake up,' and dragged me over to his side. I lay on my back and slowly spread my legs. He penetrated me. The smell of raki and sheep grew stronger. I tried to think of you. His panting sounded like the grunting of pigs. He is a real animal, a real savage. Do you remember that day when you first spoke to me, after lunch, and you said we should go for a walk through the olive trees. While we walked you picked out a tree with the thickest trunk and said that that would be our place from now on, we'd wait for each other there every day after breakfast. That day you asked me why I drew only the Virgin Mary and not also Mary Magdalene and Mary of Egypt. You spoke to me that day about their carnal experiences, about how, before they became saints, they had been whores, but I covered my ears and ran away in embarrassment. I never told you that while I was running through the olive trees, I thought Olympia was right, you really were a devil. That evening before going to bed I asked Sister Olympia if it was true that Mary Magdalene and Mary of Egypt had been whores before they were saints, she looked at me, her brows drawn, and said, 'She told you that, didn't she? They had been, but they repented. Don't tell this to the other girls. I knew that that devil would

17

bring us problems.' I avoided you for the next few days, and you paid no attention to me. But I was hurt by your inattention, I didn't want you to think that I was like the others. That day when I sat down next to you at breakfast and you got up and went to another table, I left the dining hall and went to the recreation room and began to draw, I drew Mary Magdalene, I didn't know what she looked like, but I drew her with long blond hair like yours and a red dress like yours. Then I wrote a letter to you saying I would wait for you at the olive trees. I sat down in front of the thick trunk with the picture and waited for you, I don't know how much time passed, it felt like all of eternity, and just when I thought you wouldn't come, I saw you sitting under a different tree and you were looking at the sky, and when I approached you, you didn't look at me, you kept looking up and whistling to yourself. That was the first time I saw that women also knew how to whistle through their lips, I thought only men could do that, I placed the picture in front of you and said, 'There, I've drawn Mary Magdalene.' You sat up, took the picture in your hands and looked at it silently. You can't imagine how I was dying of fear at that moment, thinking you'd tell me that it didn't look like Mary Magdalene and would throw it away. Finally, you looked into my eyes and said, 'I knew you weren't like the others. You are even better than El Greco.' In embarrassment, I quietly asked who El Greco was. You spent a long time telling me about him, and with my head leaning on your shoulder, I imagined him in Italy and in Spain, although I didn't know what those countries looked like. I don't know how you knew all those things, maybe you really were a devil, but I enjoyed listening to you. Suddenly you jumped up and told me that when you turned sixteen, and I was fifteen, we would run away from the convent, we'd go to Athens, you would work, and I would study so I could enter the Arts Academy. Then we'd run off to Spain and we'd stay and live there. We would live somewhere by the sea, I would draw, and you, you'd open a pastry shop and you would bake cookies. I began to imagine you pouring out flour, and as it falls from your hands, a white fog rises up around you, and then I see your face completely white and I began to laugh, and you were also laughing. We lay there under the tree laughing. I am laughing even now.

I had completely forgotten Mihalis; when I looked at him, he was standing over me looking bewildered. I started to laugh even louder, and he put his hand over my mouth and told me to be quiet, that it was enough for us to have one Stella, the crazy wife of the lighthouse keeper. But I couldn't stop laughing. I fell silent a moment, then I looked at Mihalis and began to cry, Irini woke up and looked at me in fright. Mihalis tried to get me to be quiet, but I cried for you, for Crete, and I cried for the Arts Academy, and Spain, I cried for the pastry shop, and the boat that would never come to Gavdos.

A SICK COUNTRY: OKSANA

This morning Igor went to summon the doctor again, the doctor told him he'd come under one condition, that we give him ten thousand drachmas; we have barely a thousand. In the end I gave him my ring, the one with the green amethyst my mother wore, she gave it to me when I turned eighteen and my grandmother had given it to her; Evgenii and I don't have children, so I wouldn't have anyone to give it to. Igor told me that when the doctor saw the ring, he said we shouldn't lock the door, he'd come that night. I spent the whole day in the house. I sat and waited. I had no strength to get up from the table. Evgenii's intermittent coughing reminded me I was still alive. I sat and waited for Igor to come. Someone knocked on the door. First lightly, and then more forcibly. I thought it was the doctor. There was no one outside. It had already grown dark. I stood for a while looking into the dark. From out of the darkness a pebble flew past me. 'Who's there?' I shouted as loud as I could. And from the darkness a man emerged, tall with a thick, black beard and a wild look, with a sheep beside him. 'What do you want?' I asked loudly. When I walked towards him, he pulled back a step and then disappeared into the darkness and the sheep disappeared with him. I stood looking into the darkness until Igor appeared; he told me to go in, it was cold out. He asked whether the doctor had come, I told him about the man with the sheep. 'That's Spiros,' he said and began to laugh loudly. 'Everyone on the island says he sleeps with it, they're never apart.' I asked how he knew what everyone on the island said since he didn't communicate with anyone, he knitted his brows and looked in confusion at the window; he said that the doctor had told him. There was something suspicious about his story. I stood there looking at him in disbelief. Suddenly he got up and said cheerily, 'I have something for you.' He pulled a white book from his pocket. 'Take it,' he said, 'this will help you learn a little Greek, so you won't be bored all the time.' I looked at the black letters on the white cover, he stood beside me and began to read: 'Petroula Psiloritis,' then with his finger he moved along the title and slowly read out: '*Arrosti Politeia*.' Then he looked at me and added, with a smile, '*The Sick Country*. Petroula Psiloritis is the pseudonym of Galatea Kazantzakis.' Before he could continue, I cut him off to ask where he got the book. 'I went by the lighthouse again today. There on the same rock as yesterday was the crazy woman. I stopped right behind her, but she didn't look at me even once, she stood about three or four hours on the rock looking at the sea. Suddenly she turned and when she saw me, she looked at me in confusion, she looked at me as if she were seeing me for the first time. When I greeted her, she began to run along the goat path that leads to the lighthouse, she was running at breakneck speed, holding the hem of her dress so she wouldn't trip, as she ran she would glance back to see whether I was following her. After she disappeared, I climbed up on the rock where she had been standing and I saw the book there.'

Quietly, almost inaudibly, I asked if one day I might go there with him, I said that I really wanted to see her. 'It's still early for that,' he said. I took the book and went off to the room where Evgenii was. He had a temperature again, and when I woke him to give him something to eat, he looked at me as if he didn't recognize me, he ate some of the fish soup and looked at me with distrust, and I had no strength to say anything to him. It was as if I had forgotten how to speak. Every so often I felt like saying, 'Arrosti politeia,' but my throat would tighten, as though it would permit nothing to come out.

The doctor didn't come.

A BOAT WITHOUT AN OAR: PENELOPE

When Irini entered the room, I was embroidering an oar for the small boat I'd embroidered on a pillow. I had been trying to finish it for a long time but kept putting it off – whenever I picked up the needle, something would interfere with my plans. When Irini entered, I set the pillow on the sewing basket by the window. Irini sat down opposite me, she had the ironic smile on her lips that she had whenever she did something naughty, her eyes sparkled, she blinked from time to time and she looked like a perfidious cat trying to take revenge. She pulled out her hands, which she had been holding behind her back, her fingers were tightened into a fist, she waved her fists several times in the air then suddenly opened them. She unfurled her fingers one by one. Ten red nails flashed in the winter sunlight that barely penetrated through the small kitchen window. Nail polish, I thought, then said aloud, 'Nail polish,' how unreal that sounded here, like a parallel universe, here the women don't know what lipstick is, or what nail polish is, the women are always dressed in black, they don't even know that any other colour exists. I finally managed to ask where she had found it. Irini hadn't stopped waving her hands in the air and that ironic smile hadn't left her lips. 'The woman with the short hair, the barbarian, gave it to me.' I couldn't take my eyes off those nails, ten little red soldiers standing in a row one beside the other. Irini no longer laughed ironically, she looked at me in confusion, she had expected me to shout and maybe go over to see the woman. I glanced towards the house, but there was no one there, it looked as if no one had lived there for years. When I looked again at Irini, the red soldiers had disappeared, she had tucked her hands between her legs, and there was fear on her face, the same fear as when Mihalis told me about the foreigners. She looks so much like him, perhaps that's why I never managed to love her. Nail polish, I hadn't heard those words since the day you came into the dining hall and whispered to me that we would meet by the olive trees after lunch. I ate so quickly that Sister Theoktisti scolded me several times, telling me not to be in such a hurry, no one was going to eat my food, but I wanted nothing but to finish as quickly as possible and run off to the olive grove. You were the only one about whom they didn't care whether you showed up for lunch. When I got to the thick trunk, you were sitting there drawing on the ground with a small stick. When you saw me, you smiled and pulled from your pocket a small bottle of red liquid. I thought it was paint, and as always, you knew then what I was thinking. You told me to sit beside you. You opened the bottle and began to colour your fingernail with the small brush. 'Nail polish,' you said, as you moved on to the next finger. This was the first time I had seen anything like it. Sometimes, when the convent was celebrating the Dormition, Sister Theoktisti let us pick roses in the courtyard, and we used them to colour our lips lightly. But without looking at me, you began to tell a story: 'One morning, when I was seven years old, my mother saw my father off to the olive factory where he worked, she washed the breakfast dishes, put a chicken and potatoes in the oven to bake. After she had baked the chicken, she went to wash up, then she put on the dress she had brought from Moscow, which she wore only on holidays. She put on red lipstick, she always wore just a touch, it was nearly imperceptible, this time she put on more than usual, she told me to go to my grandma's, she was going to Heraklion to buy red nail polish. She set off from Agia Varvara on the eleven o'clock bus and should have returned on the bus at two. Three o'clock passed, my father came home on his lunch break, we ate the chicken. Then six o'clock came, then eight, all the buses had gone. She never returned. After a few months someone at my father's factory told him that he had seen her going about the shops in Hania, wearing a silk dress the colour of cypress. Two days later someone else told him that he had seen her at the Moschato subway station in Athens, holding a large black umbrella in her right hand though it wasn't raining. A year after she left, a relative came to our house and said that he had seen my mother in Kokkinos Pirgos, not just once, he had seen her several times. He described the house, and my father and I went there just to ask her why she had left. We found the house easily; it was the only two-storey house that faced the sea. In the courtyard, lavender was growing, lots of lavender. When we stopped in front of the house a young girl came out the front door, her hair brushed the way my mother used to brush mine. When I saw the girl, I wanted to leave, but my father wouldn't let go of my hand, he said that she owed both of us an answer. My father asked the girl if her mother was there, she said she was at the neighbour's but she'd be back soon, we could come in if we wanted. That was the longest wait of my life, my father kept wiping the sweat from his forehead. I didn't want to know why she had left; I wanted to know whether she had bought the red nail polish. I thought she would come in wearing the same silk dress the colour of a ripe fig, the one she was wearing when she left, and her nails would be lacquered in red polish. She finally appeared, but it wasn't my mother. The woman really did look like her, but it wasn't my mother. When my father told her why we had come, she looked with pity at me, she went into the kitchen and brought out two pieces of lemon cake and gave them to her daughter, telling us to eat them down by the sea. We stayed with them the whole day. At that moment I wanted my mother to love lavender and to know how to make lemon cake. I wanted her to know how to laugh like this woman; the only time I saw my mother smiling was the day she told me to go to my grandmother's, that she had to go to Heraklion. We never heard anything about her again.'

When you finished telling the story, you were doing your last nail. As you lifted your head, you saw tears pouring down my face, you blew on your thumb several times, then wiped my eyes with it. To break the unbearable silence, you continued your story. 'When I turned eight, I hopped on the bus every day at eleven o'clock, I went to the harbour in Heraklion and waited for the boat from Athens, it always arrived at noon, I stood and watched the river of travellers until the last one got off. When I saw that my mother wasn't there, I returned home on the two o'clock bus, the same bus on which she never returned. I never stood in front of the boat, always off to the side, on a rock that looked directly into the passengers' exit door; I was afraid that if she got off and saw me, she'd run off again. One day while I was sitting on the rock, an older man came up to me, he told me that he watched me standing on the rock every day and that he had written a poem for me. It was Odysseus Elytis. *You have a taste of tempest on your lips – But where did you wander/All day long in the hard reverie of stone and sea? /An eagle-bearing wind stripped the hills/Stripped your longing to the bone/And the pupils of your eyes received the message of chimera/Spotting memory with foam!*[1]

You stood in the middle of the olive grove and recited 'Marina of the Rocks', but I couldn't stop crying. There were so many things I wanted to tell you, I wanted to tell you that after I learned my father had drowned, I didn't drink water for days, each gulp made me sick, and from that day on I hadn't put fish in my

---

[1] 'Marina of the Rocks' by Odysseus Elytis. Poetry International. Translation by Edmund Keeley and Philip Sherrard. From *Orientations*.

mouth, it made me feel like I was eating my father. You kept reciting, but something kept tightening in my chest, and now I was feeling that same pain.

Irini began to scream, 'Don't! Stop! Stop, please!' When I looked at her, I saw her staring in fright at my right hand, I had squeezed the pillow so hard that the needle that had been stuck in the oar of the little boat was now in my palm, blood was streaming down to my nails, in an instant my nails were also red.

* * *

Mihalis returned before sunset. Dinner was still not ready. The pillow with half an oar rested on my knees. He came in and, without speaking, sat at the table with his back to me. Irini sat opposite him. He didn't even notice her; he pulled the bottle of raki towards him and poured some in his glass. I tried to signal Irini with my eyes to go to the other room, she sat there laughing ironically at me. She looked at Mihalis and placed her hands on the table. The ten soldiers stood one beside the other, this time they looked threatening, as though they could attack at any moment. Irini did not stop her ironic laughter. Mihalis lifted his glass of raki and poured it down his throat, and only then did he notice Irini sitting across from him. I jumped up to take her into the other room and then I saw that the red soldiers were under the table, I relaxed, I felt a great sense of relief. Mihalis looked at her severely and she immediately got up from the table and went into the other room. When he is sitting at the table, we are not allowed to sit with him, 'A woman's place is beside the table, not at the table,' he would constantly repeat. He kept hoping I would give him a son, but I hadn't even wanted to give birth to Irini, every evening I had prayed that I wouldn't get pregnant so he would send me back to the convent. When I became pregnant with Irini, I knew it was the end of me, that I would never again leave Gavdos. I sat down again behind him and quietly asked him what was new. Without turning towards me, he poured himself another raki and began to speak: 'This afternoon while we were sitting in Kostas' taverna, the guy came in, the Russian. He shamelessly sat down at the middle table. When he saw that no one was coming to serve him, he loudly ordered a raki. Kostas told him it would be better if he left, that he had no place there, only islanders were welcome in the taverna. He replied that he was waiting for the doctor, he had something to discuss with him. The priest, who was sitting with me at the table playing backgammon, gave a sign to Kostas to give the guy his raki and let him wait for the doctor. He sat there and waited, but when he saw that the doctor wasn't coming, he drank up the raki and left. When he had gone, Kostas angrily told the priest that he shouldn't have served him, this would just get him used to it and he would start coming more often. The priest didn't know what to say in his own defence, so he said that he knew what he was doing, but no one believed him, we all knew that even he wasn't sure what was the right thing to do. Spiros said that he had seen the Russian standing in front of the doctor's house, they talked about something and then the doctor let him inside. Later, when the doctor arrived, the priest asked him right off what he was doing with the Russian; at first the doctor denied having seen him at all except on the day they arrived at the port in Karave. Spiros told him that he had seen them talking, and that got him flustered, he wasn't expecting that, he looked in confusion at me, then at the priest, then at Spiros, and finally he said that the Russian had come to his house begging him to go to their house and examine their friend who was seriously ill, but he had refused. None of us believed him, we know how greedy he is for money, he realised that and said he had to go, he had some work he needed to finish. When he left, the priest said we needed to keep an eye on him, he turned towards Spiros and told him to be on constant alert. Then Giorgos the lighthouse keeper came, he hadn't been to the taverna for a long time, he said that Stella was unwell again and that maybe he should listen to the doctor and maybe it would be best to send Stella to the hospital in Souda, on Crete, there was a hospital there where people like Stella were sent, he wanted to say crazy people, but he fell silent, as if the word were unpleasant for him to utter. We all kept quiet, we didn't know what to say to him, if she had only given him children…' He turned towards me, it was the first time in a long while that he had looked me in the eyes, and he said to me, 'You're all the same! All of you!'

I set the pillow on the windowsill on top of the basket with needles and thread, saying I was going to check to see how dinner was coming along. He continued to pour himself raki.

MEETING: OKSANA

Above the sea there was a white cloud that hid Crete. I opened the window and breathed deeply; the air smelled of salt. Nothing soothes my unease as much as the sea. But here, closed in the house, all I can do is remember, remember you, and think back on those long winters in Ukraine, the snow that fell for days, and you and me sitting on the floor of your father's study looking at the map he had drawn the night before. You wanted to become a cartographer like him and draw maps of undiscovered islands, but I didn't want to be anything, all I wanted was to travel. And while we were sitting there that morning, which reminds me a lot of this one, I told you that if travel is the search for one's self, I never want to find myself. You laughed aloud, I laughed too. Now I don't even know when I last laughed like that, sincerely, wholeheartedly.

Do you remember my watch with the brown wristband? It's on my wrist even today, but the day we came here it stopped working, and anyway, here you have all the time for yourself, so why would you measure it? Nothing is like it was in Ukraine. I don't even know Evgenii anymore. He is less and less present. He talked all night, but not with me, with Ruslan, a colleague who worked with us in Chernobyl. He doesn't notice when I am lying beside him or when I get up. When he is awake, he stares at a point in space and doesn't even notice my presence in the room. Sometimes I wonder why we even sleep together.

Although the calendar says it is winter, outside it looked more like spring, which I took as a call to go outside. I didn't even look

29

to see whether Igor was in the house. When I got outside, I saw the woman standing near our house, it looked like she was waiting for me. I looked into her eyes the colour of the sea; a person could easily drown in them. We stood there and looked at each other. You could hear her daughter calling to her from the house. She's always screaming. The woman set off towards her house and, without turning, went inside. I circled the house a few times, not knowing what to do. I thought about going down to the sea, but I was afraid I would run into Igor. In the end, I decided to walk to the edge of the village. I went past a house which I knew was the priest's, but except for several chickens running around the yard, I didn't see anyone. Just past the house was a small church, and in the churchyard, a cemetery. The graves were facing the sea. I saw that there was someone standing behind one of the gravestones observing me. I thought it was the man with the sheep and I hurried to the way out. As I neared the gate, I turned once more, and I saw an old woman standing there. She had long, white hair, thick white eyebrows, and her skin was white, she looked like a porcelain doll. From behind the gravestones a black tomcat leapt towards her. It also looked at me. The woman smiled at me then suddenly disappeared with the cat among the tombstones. Every few seconds I caught a glimpse of its tail from behind a grave, and the woman would wink at me from behind a tombstone and smile. When they had disappeared completely, I headed back, I didn't want Igor to see that I was out.

Igor still hadn't returned. When I climbed upstairs to the bedroom, I saw Evgenii sitting by the window looking at the sea. He didn't even turn when I came in. I took a chair and sat beside him. We looked together at the sea in silence. I wanted to ask him what was happening with us, but I couldn't, and as though he felt the same thing, he said without looking at me, 'Who knows whether we made a mistake in coming here?' He got up from his chair and lay down again on the bed. I stayed and looked at the sea and he looked at the point where he always looked. When I couldn't stand the quiet any longer, I went downstairs to wait for Igor. It had already grown dark outside, and then it began to rain. Do you remember when your father told us that islands were unpredictable, how it could easily begin to rain and then a few hours later the sun could be shining again?

I sat in the dark and listened to the rain.

A ROOM WITH A VIEW OF THE SEA: PENELOPE

Ever since the first day I came to this house I have avoided the room on the upper floor. It's the only room in the house with a view of the sea. I am not afraid of confronting the sea, I am afraid of confronting Crete. Today for the first time after so many years I looked over, across the sea, and it seemed unreal to me, as if it had never existed, as if I had never lived there, but that thought frightened me even more, because that would mean that I had never met you. Would I have thought of you at all, would I have had the courage to stand at this window if they hadn't come, the barbarians? I opened the window and breathed deeply. It smelled of salt. I felt a queasiness in my stomach, it was the smell of my father's death, the smell of your escape. I closed it quickly. I looked once again towards Crete, I wanted to assure myself that it was really there, that it truly existed. The white cloud that had been above the sea, hiding it, slowly pulled away, and there before me was the view I so feared. I couldn't take my eyes off it, I wanted to make up for all these years. It is winter, I thought. Psiloritis must be covered in snow. And suddenly all the snow swept inside me. From the weight of the snow I couldn't move from the chair. I sat and looked.

The door behind me slowly opened. I sensed several hesitant steps approaching me. It was Mihalis. His eyes held the same fear as on the day the barbarians came. He was afraid of this room perhaps even more than I was. Do you remember how you told me that the day your mother left, your father called some workmen to block up the only window in the house that looked towards the sea, because he was afraid that you'd run off just like her? She had always sat at the window and looked out. What Mihalis feared most of all was that I'd come into this room and when I saw the sea, I would want to run away. But boats come here so rarely that even if I wanted to, I couldn't.

'Where is Irini?' he asked to break the uncomfortable silence. 'At school,' I answered. He sat on the iron bed, on the same bed on which he was born, on which his mother died, the bed on which Irini was born and on which I will most likely die, too. This is his mother's room. He had told me that his father was a sailor and rarely came home. Once he brought his mother an umbrella the colour of ripe melon. She never used it, she rarely left the house, but she kept the umbrella in the wooden cupboard in this room, among her dowry items. Whenever she saw a boat, she would open the window and begin to wave it, she would wave until the boat had passed. He came less and less often, and she stood more and more often at the window waving. One day a sailor who had been with him on the same boat told her that he wasn't returning and how they had stopped somewhere in Portugal because of a storm and they were sitting in a café in the harbour when her husband told them he was going to take a leak but never came back. At first, they thought he was drunk and had fallen into the sea and drowned, or that someone had killed him thinking he had money on him, but several months later when they stopped again in the same port, they ran into him in the café from which he had left and never returned; they hardly recognised him, he was a new man, he told them he had got married to a Portuguese woman. That evening when he went off to pee, instead of going back inside, he set off down the street and along the way he met a woman with an umbrella the colour of ripe melon, he set off after her, followed her to her house –

she was a widow, with no children. He begged a sailor from Gavdos to tell his wife not to wait for him. As the sailor was leaving, he gave him his old wedding ring. When Mihalis's mother heard this, she closed herself up completely in this room and never left, she got out of bed only when she heard a boat's horn, she closed the shutters so as not to see the boat. One day when Mihalis came into her room to leave food for her, the window was wide open, she was holding the umbrella in her right hand, but she was dead.

He sat and looked out the window, but not at the sea, he was looking at Crete; the only time he had visited Crete was the day he came to get me at the convent. There was no sign of remorse in his face, nor of happiness. He noticed I was looking at him and he smiled in embarrassment, I have never seen him laugh. 'Strange things happened today. This morning the Russian came to the taverna again. He sat down and ordered a raki. When Kostas brought it to him, he asked when the doctor would come. The priest asked him why he was always looking for the doctor. He didn't answer. He kept drinking and looking at the door. He drank it in two gulps. And just when he wanted to order another, Spiros came in and said that he had seen the doctor getting into a fisherman's boat. He had a suitcase in his hand. We all jumped up, the Russian did too, he threw some drachmas on the table and flew out the door. The doctor had run off. The priest said he had always seemed suspicious to him, and that he was probably the one who brought them to the island, that it couldn't possibly be a coincidence that they had arrived the same day. While we were sitting there, we heard a scream from the taverna's courtyard. It was Katerina, Kostas' wife. We all went outside; she was standing there terrified, looking at a dead snake. The priest said it was probably that woman, the Russian, who had thrown it into the courtyard, and that she and her husband had probably been together.' If this had taken place in winter, just a month ago, they would likely have blamed Stella, the lighthouse keeper's crazy wife. They tied every strange thing that happened on the island to Stella, maybe someone might have thought of Aliki, the herbalist, but they were afraid of her and her powers and they didn't even want to mention her name because it might get her riled up.

The door of the room opened and the two of us looked at each other in fright. It was Irini. She stood there in the half-open doorway and looked at us laughing with her ironic grin.

THE FLOOD: OKSANA

It rained all night. It was even raining in my dream. Igor checks the door and the windows and adds: 'This is nothing, wait till you see how much it'll rain, you'll see later what kind of rain will fall.' During the night there is more rain, it rains harder and harder. I open my eyes to a room full of water. Everything is under water: the table, the chairs, the beds… Wherever I look, water everywhere. Igor lifts Evgenii and me onto the bed and begins to drag us towards the door and out of the house. Outside, there is nothing but water. 'Look, even the stars and the moon are gone, the water has swallowed them up, too,' Evgenii says. 'Didn't I tell you the whole island would drown?' Igor adds and he begins to row with his hands. I remain silent and look at the sky, from which the rain keeps pouring. Evgenii looks down at the water and says nostalgically, 'Everything has drowned. We shouldn't have come to the island. Now we have nothing. What little we had, we've lost.' I want to tell him that we have our words, with them we will create everything from the beginning, but I am afraid to say it aloud, I don't want to break the silence and leave us without that as well. 'Hang on a little, it will be dawn soon and we'll find a dry place to settle in,' says Igor.

When I opened my eyes, it was already day. The sun was shining brightly. There was no trace of the rain. I was no longer certain whether it had rained at all or been only a dream. Even my dreams are different here from my dreams in Ukraine. I went into Igor's room to see whether he had returned. His bed was made. He had not come back at all. When I went to the room I share with Evgenii, I found Evgenii sitting up. When I stood beside him, he didn't budge, he sat and looked at the point in front of him. 'Igor didn't return last night.' 'Who's Igor?' he asked me with indifference. I was expecting him to ask where I had been all night. Why I hadn't slept beside him. I wanted to tell him that while waiting for Igor to return, I had fallen asleep at the table, I wanted to tell him my dream, but he kept looking at that point in front of him, muttering something to himself, quietly, as if my presence bothered him. When I went downstairs, Igor was sitting at the table acting as if nothing had happened. There was a woven basket covered with a white cloth napkin in front of him. 'Where were you all night?' 'By the lighthouse.' 'What were you doing there all night?' 'I went in the morning to catch fish for lunch. The crazy woman was there. She was sitting on a rock looking towards the sea. She was wearing some kind of cape over her black dress and had a hat on her head.' 'What colour was the cape?' I asked because I wanted to know everything, I live for these stories he tells me, it's the only way I feel that I am still alive, that there's something happening in the world. 'Red.' 'That's an unusual colour for the island women.' He just nodded but said nothing. 'This basket was next to her,' he said, gesturing towards the basket on the table. He pulled off the white cloth, and inside was a loaf of white bread, olives, dried figs and a piece of cheese. When I saw the food, I realised that the previous day I had eaten nothing at all. Ever since we came here, all we eat is the fish that Igor catches, it's the only food we live on. But at that moment I was hungrier for stories, for life, I told him to tell me more. 'Sometime around noon a wind came up. The crazy woman left the basket on a rock and began running along the goat path towards the lighthouse. I took the basket and ran after her to give it to her. I caught up to her near the entrance to the lighthouse, she turned and screamed in fright. Her cape fell off, but she kept running. She left the door open. I left her cape and

37

the basket on the doorstop and I returned to the rock. As it grew darker, it began to rain harder and harder. I didn't want to come back without having caught a single fish for dinner. At one point it was raining so hard, I decided to go home. When I passed by the lighthouse, I saw the door was still open, and the basket and cape were still by the door, I pulled aside the cloth and saw there was food inside. I took the basket. I couldn't return empty-handed. It was raining so hard that the path wasn't even visible. I went into the yard, there just beside the lighthouse is the house that belongs to the lighthouse keeper and his crazy wife. I saw that part of the house was used as a barn; I went inside and hid behind a bundle of hay. I fell asleep from the warmth. I was awakened in the morning when I heard the lighthouse keeper talking to the goats. I knew it was him; no one lives there except the two of them. I didn't see his face, I just heard his voice. I hid behind the hay so he wouldn't see me, and when I saw that he was leaving, I waited a bit and then I went out into the yard. She was there. The crazy woman. She was standing there looking at the sun. Her eyes were closed. She was wearing the red cape she had had on the previous day. I slowly passed by her, but she didn't notice me. The only thing I was worried about was meeting the lighthouse keeper and for him to see the basket and think I was stealing.' He took a deep breath and fell silent. He was silent and looking in front of him. I waited for him to continue the story, but he turned to me and asked, 'What about you... how did you pass the time?' I wanted to ask how I should pass it, since I don't go out at all during the day, but then I remembered the strange woman in the cemetery with her cat, and my desire to learn who she was greater than my fear that he would chastise me for going out. I quickly told him about my meeting the woman, but he only shifted position on his chair and began speaking: 'At the edge of the village there's a house. The people on the island call that part of the village the women's village because of the albino twins. They're the oldest inhabitants of the island. No one knows exactly how old they are. People say that twins were often born in their family, but they're the only set of twins in which both survived. Whenever twins were born, the second-born was thrown in the well, people thought it was evil, there shouldn't exist two of the same people in the world. They're the only two to survive and so everyone on the island is afraid of them, especially of Aliki, she's the second-born, she's the one you saw, the one born first is Kiki, no one can even remember the last time they saw her. What made people even more afraid of them is that when they were born, they were white, their eyebrows were white, their eyelashes, the bits of hair on their head. They rarely came out during the daytime, but at night they wandered around the island laughing loudly. Whenever people heard them laughing, they'd go inside their houses so they wouldn't run into them. One evening, apparently, when the priest was eleven years old, he was going by the beach at Sarakiniko and he heard loud laughter, he knew it was them, he climbed up on a rock and saw two white heads in the sea. There was a full moon. The two girls came out of the sea and began to chase each other along the beach, and the priest sat there watching them with curiosity. They were all white, even their pubic hair was white. It was the first time in his life he had seen a naked female body. He sat on the rock and watched until he noticed something strange – both girls had six toes on each foot. When he saw that, the priest became so frightened that he screamed at the top of his lungs, the two girls paid no attention to his scream, but continued chasing each other and laughing. That's supposedly when the priest decided to become a monk, and when he turned fourteen he was sent to a monastery on Crete, where he remained until he turned seventeen, when he decided to complete theological school and become a priest and return to the island. When he returned, nothing was the same, Aliki had become an herbalist and everyone went to her for medicines, she gathered herbs during the day up on Tripiti, but Kiki no longer went out, she sat all the time closed in at home. People say that after the Second World War something happened to the twins, they lived in separate rooms and didn't want to see each other. Kiki survives on whatever Aliki feels compelled to give to her.'

When he finished his story, Igor said he was tired and that he was going to rest in his room. I pulled the olives and cheese from the basket, set them on a plate and took them to Evgenii. When I entered the room I found him sitting by the window talking to himself. I left the food on the floor beside him and, without saying a word to him, I left.

KISS: PENELOPE

These past few days I've been tired all the time. My breasts are swollen. But the pains in my lower back were how I knew for sure that I was pregnant again. It was the same when I was pregnant with Irini. Do you remember when we sat under our olive tree and you asked me whether I ever wanted to have children? I didn't know what to answer. I didn't know, in fact, whether I wanted them or not. Up until that moment I had never thought about it. Until then I hadn't even had a crush on anyone. Until your arrival, I was afraid of life, I was afraid of leaving the convent, that is why I wanted to stay there forever. To look after the young wards. You looked at me intently. You waited for an answer. I told you that I wanted to have a child, but not a husband. That I never wanted to get married. The thing about the husband was true. You smiled. You were pleased with my answer. So was I. What about you, do you want children? I asked. No, I'm afraid that like my mother, one day I'd go off and buy nail polish and I would never return. In fact, I'm sure that's how it would be. But I want to have a husband. Not one, I want many men, you said. I didn't like your answer at all. I was jealous. I wanted you for myself, I was afraid that if you loved a man, I would lose you forever. But you just smiled at me and told me not to be stupid, that the man for whom you would leave me didn't exist. To calm me, you knelt and stroked my face, you brushed aside the lock of hair that fell across my cheek and you kissed me. Yes, you kissed me. Not on my cheek. You kissed me on the lips. Like men and women kiss. Like in a movie. Once when I got sick, when no one knew what was wrong with me, when none of Sister Erotea's teas helped, nor the doctor in Mires, I was sent to the hospital in Heraklion. I went with Sister Erotea, who, before joining the convent, had been a nurse in Heraklion, she knew the doctors. We were finished earlier than expected, and Sister Erotea said that the cinema was showing a rerun of the film *Stella*, that the last time she had seen it was about twenty years before in Athens when she visiting some relatives at Christmas and they took her to see it. It was the first and last time that I ever went to the cinema. Sister Erotea said that Sister Theoktisti mustn't know, that it would be our secret. I have never forgotten that kiss when Giorgos Funtas was going to stab Melina Mercouri with a knife, and she told him to kiss her. I saw Sister Erotea wipe away tears during that scene, but I watched open-mouthed at Melina Mercouri begging Giorgos Funtas to kiss her. And then when you kissed me, I felt more shame than ever before. After that kiss I did not enter the convent chapel all week, I felt ashamed before the Virgin Mary, yet in secret I deeply desired you to kiss me again, but you acted as if nothing had happened.

Irini was at school. This was my chance to go to Aliki, the herbalist. When I got to her place, the door to her house was closed. I knocked. From the other side I heard a voice calling out, 'She's not here, check the graveyard.' That was Kiki, her twin sister. Kiki never goes out. Not even Mihalis has ever seen her. While I was leaving the yard, I felt as if someone were standing behind me, watching, but no one was there. Most likely Kiki was watching me through a window, hidden behind the curtain. There was no one at the graveyard. A chill went through me. This child must not be born. I have never loved Irini as a mother should love her child. I've always seen in her an obstacle to my escape. I didn't have your mother's bravery. Whenever I thought of fleeing, I would look at Irini and the weight of my conscience would overwhelm me. I cannot leave her alone on the island.

In the lower part of my belly I felt intense cramps. I don't know whether it was from the pregnancy or from the thought that I would never be able to escape. Just then, out from behind a gravestone I saw a black tail. It was Kallias. Aliki's cat. I walked again among the tombstones and I saw Aliki bent over a grave gathering some type of herb. She looked at me as if she had been expecting me. 'That's what I came for.' I gestured towards the herbs in her hand. 'I know,' she said. She looked at me and laughed. She is the only person on the island who laughs. There was a warmth in her smile. I never understood why everyone was afraid of her. From a bag she was carrying she pulled out a folded paper packet, she gave it to me and said, 'You put it in with the tips of your fingers and drink it like tea.' I quickly tucked the packet down into my bra. 'Make sure you don't use too much, you know what could happen.' I nodded yes then hurried to leave before anyone saw me. This is a death-inducing herb. All the women on the island know about it. It is a secret that the women pass on from one to another in case they unwillingly get pregnant. Aliki gathers it from the graveyards, it sprouts among the graves, it feeds on the bones of the dead. Once, long ago, Katerina, the wife of the taverna owner, told me about the herb, saying that after I drank the tea, I'd bleed a short time and then I'd lose the unwanted embryo. As I was hurrying home to do it before Irini got home, I ran into that woman. The Russian. With my finger, I pointed to the lemon tree, she looked surprised as if she hadn't seen it before. She went over to it and plucked a lemon, she tentatively handed it to me. Her hands were tender, I hadn't felt such warmth in a long time. We stood there and looked at each other. I wanted so much to tell her that I knew how things were for her, but I wasn't sure she would understand me. She had the most beautiful facial features. You must look like this too, I thought to myself. But as if reading my thoughts, she shyly lowered her head. Then Spiros appeared behind her with his sheep. He looked at me with reproach. When she saw him, she ran frightened into her house. He gestured with his head for me to leave as well. Ever since the first day I saw him, I've felt uncomfortable in his presence. When I set off, I saw that the woman was standing in the window looking at me. I squeezed the lemon tightly in my hand.

DEATH UNDER THE LEMON TREE: OKSANA

Evgenii is dead. I spent the night at the table again. I did not want to sleep beside him. Day by day Evgenii was becoming stranger and more distant. When I went into the room he was sitting, staring at the point in space in front of him. The plate of food lay untouched. When I asked him why he hadn't eaten, he began to laugh. I asked again and he laughed even louder. His gaze was odd, unfocused somehow, as if he weren't looking at me. I tried to get him to be quiet, I told him to stop laughing, but at every word I said he laughed even more. I pulled out the pillow he was propped up against and I began to hit him with it. Even then he kept laughing. I struck him as hard as I could. I was enraged by his laughter. I was hitting to hurt him, to get him to stop. Suddenly he grew tired and lay on his back, and when I started to cry, he began to laugh again. This time he laughed as if he were also crying. I couldn't endure that horrible laughter. I pressed the pillow against his face and began to push with all my strength. He didn't stop laughing. When I moved the pillow aside, he was already dead. His eyes were open. I took a blanket and covered his head. I didn't want to remember him like this. I went downstairs to wait for Igor. It was growing dark outside. Igor didn't come. In my head was ringing, 'So who's Igor?' I was no longer certain whether Igor really existed or whether in my solitude I was speaking with someone like I speak to you. I no longer knew what was real and what was make-believe. I looked towards the window; it was already night. I was surprised when I saw my face in the glass. I had already forgotten what I looked

45

like. I had more and more white hair on my head, I had black circles under my eyes, I looked as if someone had pulled me from a flood, like the one in my dream. Is that me? I looked at myself in the glass and I laughed. Do I exist? Someone knocked on the door. I thought it was Igor. That he had been sitting in front of the window the whole time looking at me. I was afraid that he would think I had also gone crazy. I stood and opened the door. There was no one there. I quietly asked, 'Igor, is that you?' But instead of an answer, a rock hit my forehead. It was that man with the sheep. He stood in the darkness shouting 'Φύγετε! ... Φύγετε! Τρελοί ξένοι! Go away! ... Go away! You crazy foreigners!' I understood that. I began to laugh. He looked at me in confusion. I laughed at the top of my lungs. Tears rolled down my cheeks from laughter. He became frightened and ran away, disappearing in the darkness. I stood there laughing until I was exhausted. I sat on the stoop. My body suddenly became unbearably heavy. I couldn't move.

Igor didn't appear.

DEATH UNDER THE LEMON TREE: PENELOPE

I didn't see him even once. I thought he was something dreamt up by the people on the island, just like I thought at first that the crazy wife of the lighthouse keeper was make-believe. This morning they buried him, over there beside the lemon tree. Mihalis told me that the others were also sick and would also die. The news about his death spread quickly across the island. The men stayed in the taverna all day deciding what to do. Mihalis returned home late at night. The priest, he told me, had said that they'd been living peacefully long enough, but this was a terrible transgression; everyone should be patient and give him a few days to think of what needed to be done. I wasn't afraid of illness, I was afraid of the child I was carrying in my belly. This child must not be born. I hadn't managed to make tea from the herbs that Aliki had given me because Irini had returned home early from school. Mihalis saw that I was worried, but he tied my worry to the death of the Russian. 'The priest will come up with a solution, and if he doesn't, we will. They need to leave the island.' I don't want them to go. I am afraid that if that woman leaves, you will too. This time for good. With her here, you came back again to me. Life without that woman, without you, is unthinkable for me on the island. I pressed my hand under the pillow, with the tip of my fingers I touched the paper bundle, if they leave, I will drink all of it, death is the only way to get off this island. 'He came to the taverna, too,' said Mihalis. 'Who?' I asked quickly before he noticed my hand under the pillow. 'The Russian. After he buried the other guy, he came to

47

the taverna. He sat at the table he always sits at whenever he comes. He ordered a raki. Kostas didn't give it to him. The priest asked him ironically whether he was waiting for the doctor to bring him to his friend. We all laughed. He got up and left. After he went out, Spiros said that the Russian had earlier been going frequently to the lighthouse, over where the crazy woman stands, but now he sees him more and more often going over to Kastri. The priest told Spiros not to let him out of his sight and to keep following him.'

Suddenly Mihalis said he was tired, that he wanted to sleep. He turned over and began to snore. I dragged myself from the bed and sat by the window.

WALLS: OKSANA

Ever since the day we buried Evgenii over there by the lemon tree, I've been avoiding the upstairs room. I'm not afraid of facing his death, I don't even feel guilty, I know that he would have done the same thing had he been in my place. I am afraid of facing the sea. When we buried Evgenii, we buried our last hope that we would leave the island. Now my days are reduced to waiting, waiting for Igor to come, it is only his stories that make me feel I am still alive.

This morning Igor left early. I spent the day at the table. It is so quiet here that a person could easily forget to speak. From time to time I hear your voice, quiet, a child's voice, reciting:

With no consideration, no pity, no shame,/they've built walls around me, thick and high.

And I shout aloud: *But I never heard the builders, not a sound./Imperceptibly they have closed me off from the outside world.*[2] The words come ringing from me, and I no longer know whether I am saying them, or whether I am hearing you.

Igor came back just before sunset. He was holding two fish in his hand, still alive, and an octopus. He handed me the octopus and said with a smile, 'Let's celebrate a little.' We were silent throughout dinner. He didn't once mention Evgenii. As if he had never existed. From time to time I would look towards the lemon tree, but he would catch my gaze and smile at me. I wanted to tell him that since we buried Evgenii beneath the tree, three new

---

[2] 'Walls' by Constantine P. Cavafy, translated by Edmund Keeley and Philip Sherrad.

lemons had ripened, but I was afraid to say his name, just as I was afraid to say yours in front of Evgenii, because I was no longer sure what was real and what was make-believe. The making up of stories is an act of loneliness, a need for dialogue, the person who makes up a story must be very lonely.

After dinner Igor lit a cigarette. I wanted to ask him where he got the cigarettes, but I was afraid of his answer – I sometimes think that he has been living a life outside of these thick walls this whole time and that Evgenii and I were some kind of experiment – but he somehow read my thoughts and began speaking. 'I went to the taverna this morning. I was sitting at the same table I always sit at when I'm there. After Evgenii's death, the islanders are even more afraid of us. I asked Kostas, the taverna owner, for a raki; while he was deciding whether to give it to me, the priest signalled him to make me leave. Kostas is a newcomer like us. From Crete. No one knows his real name. His wife Katerina's father opened the taverna. At that time there were more people living on Gavdos, it was before they began leaving the island, before everyone forgot them. It was the only taverna, and at noon men from all parts of the island gathered there. Kostas, the old owner, went every week to Chania on Crete to get supplies. As he walked around the market, he would always see a ragged, starving child begging. Everyone kicked the child and made fun of him. The old Kostas was the only one who gave him a few drachmas. One day, one of the vendors in the market told him that the boy's parents had fallen ill with leprosy and had been sent to Spinalonga, which at that time was a leper colony. Everyone in the market thought that the boy also had leprosy because he had sores on his elbows and knees. Kostas took the child to the doctor, the same doctor who decided who would be sent to Spinalonga. After an examination, the doctor told him that the boy did not have leprosy, the sores around his eyes and elbows were from psoriasis and that many people had been mistakenly sent to Spinalonga because the doctors often confused leprosy with psoriasis. The old Kostas had two daughters, Rhea and Katerina, he took the child with him to the island to help out in the taverna and he adopted him as the son he didn't have. The child was the same age as Katerina. Rhea was four years older. When he brought the child to the island, and after they had bathed him and dressed him in the clean clothes Kostas had bought for him in the market, the child said that from then on he wanted to be called Kostas after old Kostas, who had saved his life. The child grew up with Rhea and Katerina. Rhea had never looked at him as a brother, she had always seen him as an opportunity for marriage. At that time people had started to leave the island and fewer and fewer people remained. When Kostas turned seventeen, the old Kostas told him that he would leave him the taverna and that as soon as the snow melted on Psiloritis, in the spring, he and Katerina would marry. Rhea, hurt by her father's decision to break tradition and marry off the younger daughter first, climbed into the boat that belonged to old Kostas and set off to escape to Crete. For three days and three nights they searched for her. On the fourth day she was found half frozen in the middle of the sea, barely showing signs of life. She was brought back to the island and soon fell ill with tuberculosis. She died in spring when the snow melted on Psiloritis.'

Here Igor paused. The two of us were silent. I was thinking of Rhea in the middle of the sea and I thought of you as well, you sitting beside me listening to the story. Igor took a few puffs on his cigarette and continued: 'When I left the taverna, I set off to the lighthouse. The whole way, I sensed that Spiros was following me, with his sheep. On the rock below the lighthouse she was standing there, the crazy woman. When I drew nearer, she didn't move. She was standing there looking out at the sea.

She was dressed in white, a summer dress, her hair was down, from time to time when the wind blew, her hair ruffled, giving off a scent of jasmine. She was barefoot. She was standing on the rock, the sea striking her bare feet. I have never seen such a beautiful woman. Her eyebrows were thick, her look wild, I know that that snoop Spiros is also enchanted by her. Suddenly in the distance you could hear a boat's horn, and she began to run scared towards the lighthouse. While she was running along the goat path, the wind lifted her dress, and she ran with her arms stretched out in front of her, as if she were held by an invisible rope. After she had vanished completely, I turned towards Spiros, who was only a few steps from me; when I set off towards him, he began to run away, he was running along the rocks with the sheep. On the rock next to the one he had stood on, I noticed he had forgotten his tobacco, that's where these cigarettes are from.'

He gave a half smile and took another long drag. I was pleased with the story. Suddenly that day passed at the table had given me a thought. I took one of the already rolled cigarettes. We smoked and looked at the lemon tree.

BETRAYAL: PENELOPE

This morning Irini didn't go to school. Someone knocked on the door before sunrise. Mihalis immediately jumped up, he told me not to get up and to stay in bed. After a short time, he came into the room and told me to get dressed and go to the kitchen. It was the priest. He was sitting at the table in the kitchen, he apologised to me for waking us so early but it was important. I put two glasses of raki on the table and Mihalis told me to leave, if he needed me he'd call. I stood behind the door and listened. After pouring the raki down his throat, the priest began: 'Last night Spiros came to see me with his sheep. He told me that after the Russian left the taverna, he set off to the lighthouse. Stella was standing on one of the rocks, she was waiting for him. Spiros says that she's not at all crazy, she pretends to be, and that he had seen them together before. She always waits for him on the same rock. When Stella noticed that Spiros was also there behind her, she began acting like she hadn't noticed anyone. The Russian realised they weren't alone, there was someone else there, and he stayed a few metres away from her. After a while Stella began running off in fright towards the lighthouse. The Russian drew near him and said something unintelligible in the language the barbarians speak. Spiros threw himself at him, but the guy didn't give up, so they fought, and when Spiros pulled a knife from his belt, the Russian got scared and ran off along the path Stella had taken. It was when Spiros had set off on the road to Kastri that he noticed that the Russian had stolen his tobacco.' Here the priest fell silent. I heard Mihalis pour him some more raki. The priest remained silent a moment, but when he saw that Mihalis wasn't going to say anything, he continued: 'But that's not all.' The priest paused again, as if creating suspense on purpose. Mihaliṣ gets riled up easily, and it was if he were waiting for that. At one point I heard Mihalis bang the table. 'Spiros also said…' the priest slowly began, 'he's been following the Russian for quite some time, and in addition to Stella, the Russian has been seeing another woman.' I almost gave myself away, I nearly bumped into the door trying to get closer. 'The teacher. He's been seeing the teacher. During the day he goes to the lighthouse and sees Stella, but as soon as it gets dark he goes to Kastri to the teacher's. One evening when it was raining, the Russian was coming back from the lighthouse. He had only caught one fish all day. But the fish was a large one, it must have been about two or three kilos. It was raining so hard that nothing was visible. Spiros was walking behind him. At some point the sheep began to bleat from exhaustion and the Russian realized that he was being followed. The Russian began to walk faster, knowing that this guy with the sheep couldn't catch up to him. At some point Spiros completely lost sight of him. He decided not to follow him to Vatsiana, but to go home. When he entered Kastri it was already late at night. It was still raining. He passed by the school to ask the teacher whether she needed help, but there in front of the door, he saw the Russian. He was standing there debating whether to knock on the school door. After deliberating quite some time, he gathered his courage and knocked on the door, first quietly then with more force. No one opened it. The Russian was turning to go when the teacher opened the door. It was Sunday. The teacher had been bathing. Her hair was still wet. He said something to her, and she shook her head several times, flicking off drops of water. The teacher opened the door wide so the Russian could go in, then she went into the courtyard, looked to the left and the right, and then lowered the bar to lock the door. The Russian stayed with her until dawn. As soon as the sun was shining, the teacher went out into the yard, looked left and right and gave the Russian a sign to leave. In his hand he was holding a large wooden basket covered with a white cloth.'

The priest again fell silent. Mihalis was also silent. I dragged myself into my room and lay down on the bed. This meant only one thing: Irini would no longer be going to school. And the little free time I had for myself, for us, the time in which I could remember, I would have no longer. At the same time, I felt sorry for the teacher. I imagine her entering the empty school and seeing that her only student is not there. Ah, but you know nothing about her. Two years ago, the priest sent a letter to Athens asking them to send a teacher because there was a child on Gavdos. After several months of correspondence, a letter came saying that a teacher would arrive at the beginning of September. We all went down to the harbour in Karave to welcome her. From out of the boat stepped a young woman, thirty years old, who said her name was Zoe, that she was from Corinth and that she had been sent from Athens to be the teacher. That same evening in Kastri the priest organized a party in her honour. Tables had been set up in the schoolyard, Mihalis roasted a lamb, Spiros and Giorgos the lighthouse keeper took out their instruments, and again, after a long time, life flowed on Gavdos. Everyone was delighted with Zoe's arrival. There had been no students for years in the school. The three classrooms had been arranged so that classes could be held in one of them, a second was turned into a place for the teacher to live. After a week everyone forgot about the teacher and returned to their lives. Irini was her only hope, her only contact with people. Even I hadn't been to the school since that evening.

BETRAYAL: OKSANA

Igor came home sometime after midnight. The previous day he had suggested that I sleep in his room, and he would sleep upstairs. I was getting ready to lie down when he came in, I thought that he wasn't going to come home at all, that maybe there had again been bad weather by the lighthouse and he had once again taken refuge somewhere. He entered the room without knocking, he seemed frightened, it was the first time I had seen fear in his face. He told me to sit on the bed, that there was something important he had to tell me. He sat beside me and took my hand. He had never touched me before. This must really be something serious, I thought. But I am incapable of feeling fear, or any other emotion. All I felt was curiosity. Igor was silent. I drew nearer to him; I had the impression that he wasn't even aware of me. I pulled my hand from his and then he remembered I was there beside him. 'Aliki is dead,' he said at last. I didn't reply, I wasn't even that surprised. All I wanted was for him to keep talking.

This morning Kiki found her on the doorstep. Her cat was lying beside her. Kiki brought Aliki inside, placed her on the bed and waited for it to grow dark so she could go out. This whole time the cat lay on Aliki's stomach, unmoving, as if it too were dead. When it finally grew dark, Kiki set off to find the priest. When she opened the front door, the cat flew outside ahead of her. It was lost forever in the darkness.

Kiki first went to the church to look for the priest, and when she saw he wasn't there, she went to his home, but he wasn't there either. She set off for the taverna, because after the church and his home, it was the third place she might find him. For forty-five years she hadn't left her home. As she walked, she was amazed at how much the island had changed since the day she had closed herself in forever. Nothing was the same. Houses were abandoned, there was no longer anyone to run away and lock themself inside when they saw her and Aliki. As she drew near the taverna, Spiros flew in and told them that Aliki was coming. Everybody froze in fear. Kiki stood there in front of them in a white linen dress, with straps but no sleeves. Her white hair fell to her waist. Her skin was so white it seemed it would break if you touched it. Everyone looked at her in silence. She also remained silent, searching with her gaze for the priest. When she had last seen him, he had been a child, but he was now a grandfather. She recognized him by his cassock, and she said to him, 'After all, Aliki went first.' She said this and turned to go, while everyone continued staring at her in fright. 'Aliki is dead,' the priest said, and everyone began to cross themselves. 'This is Kiki,' he added, and people crossed themselves even more. The priest set off after her. Along the way they didn't exchange a single word. From time to time Kiki would say, 'After all, she went first.'

During the winter of 1944, as the islanders were preparing to sleep, Aliki and Kiki were preparing for their walk. While the people of Crete were fighting fiercely against the Germans, the people of Gavdos got most of their information about the war from the fishermen. Just as Aliki and Kiki reached the mountain, they heard a loud bang. The whole mountain shook. Around them there were shouts, voices calling out in panic for help. Aliki and Kiki stood among the pines and giggled. Suddenly all these people were near, gas lamps in their hands to find the path more easily. When the people saw the two twins, everyone stopped and looked at them in amazement. Aliki and Kiki were also stunned, it wasn't clear to them either what was happening. And as they stood there looking at each other in amazement, someone shouted, 'Up there, on the summit, there's smoke!' The crowd ran in the direction of the smoke, Aliki and Kiki stood there dazed a bit longer and then set off after them. People were coming out from the big cloud of smoke with cans of food and camouflage tarps. When Aliki and Kiki got closer, they saw it was a German airplane. As the smoke began to dissipate, Kiki joined the others and also grabbed some cans of food and tarps. Aliki didn't move at all, she stood there looking at the dead bodies of the German soldiers. With her arms full, Kiki ran towards the village and yelled at Aliki not just to stand there but to go and take something too. Suddenly a deathly quiet set in. Everyone had run away, only Aliki continued to stand there. She saw something no one else had seen. She returned home when the sun was up. It was the first time the twins had been apart. Aliki had a wound on her right arm. Concerned about her injury, people forgot to ask what kept her so long. From that day, Aliki began to go about in daytime, and Kiki at night. The islanders called the twins day and night. It wasn't clear to anyone what had happened that night when Aliki had remained alone. After that, the twins not only moved about the island separately, but their laughter was no longer heard, their silence frightened the islanders even more. One morning before the sun was up, Kiki was returning from her night walk and as she moved through the pines, she saw Aliki climb quickly up the goat path that led to an abandoned village. Kiki followed her the whole way. Aliki entered one of the abandoned houses. A half hour later, she left. Kiki had been standing the whole time hidden in one of the other abandoned houses that looked directly into the house Aliki had entered. Outside, dawn had already broken, and while it was increasingly painful for Kiki, she was prepared to see it through to the end. When Aliki reached the end of the village, Kiki went inside the abandoned house. She finally saw what it was that had come between the twin sisters. In one corner, under a window, lay a man. The man was naked to his waist, all he had on were his army pants. One of his arms and his head were wound with bandages. Her whole world was destroyed. Her sister had betrayed her for an ordinary man. She moved listlessly through the pines, she didn't notice that it was already day, she moved like a bat set loose into daylight. Somewhere near the edge of the forest she saw Aliki run breathlessly towards her. When Aliki had returned home she had seen that Kiki's bed was empty, she had looked for her throughout the house and yard, and when she had seen that she wasn't there, it occurred to her that perhaps she hadn't returned at all. While they stood looking at each other, Aliki saw the destroyed world in Kiki's eyes. As they were returning to Vatsiana, Aliki told her everything. That night while they were grabbing canned goods and tarpaulins, Aliki saw that one of the two Germans outside the plane was still alive, and from time to time he tried to give her a sign with his fingers that he was alive. When everyone had gone, Aliki had brought him to the abandoned village, because it was only there that she knew no one would find him, not even the shepherds who climbed all day about Tripiti. The following day when she went to visit him, she thought she would find him dead, but he was still alive. She began to bring him food and water once a day, and along the way as she went to him, she gathered the herbs that the two of them had gathered with their grandmother when they were children. From the herbs she began to make medicines and balms. The German got stronger by the day. With the little Greek he knew, he told her that as soon as he felt he could move, the two of them would flee. At this Kiki became even more despondent, she had always thought that like her, Aliki was content to remain on the island forever and enjoy the feeling of being someone who strikes fear in other people. When they entered Vatsiana, Kiki, to Aliki's surprise, told her that she wouldn't reveal her secret to anyone. Happy that, in the end, she had accepted it, Aliki promised her that as soon as she got to Germany, she would do everything she could to make it possible for Kiki to come to her there, and they would again walk together at night. And the two of them giggled. From that morning on, Aliki went out by day to visit the German, and Kiki at night. He didn't even know that there were two different women. The two of them bound his wounds, fed him and helped him walk. One evening before Kiki went out, Aliki told her not to go anywhere, the day for escape had come. The German was no longer in the house, he was waiting for her down at the harbour in Karave. After midnight a fisherman would come and ferry them to Agia Roumeli on Crete. Then Kiki felt jealous, what if Aliki fled and never returned? Kiki would remain on the island her whole life waiting for Aliki to return. She would never come. Whoever leaves never returns. Kiki went outside and saw a child playing, and when the child saw her, he turned white with fear. 'What's your name?' she asked him. 'Spiros,' said the child. 'How old are you?' 'Five,' said the child. 'Go run about the houses and say that there's a German down below in Karave harbour.' The child ran from house to house and in a short time all the men of the village had gathered and set off for Karave. When the German saw the enraged villagers coming, he took the pistol from his belt and shot himself. Aliki never forgave Kiki's betrayal. The story of the soldier who recovered, the one Aliki had raised from the dead, spread across Gavdos and quickly reached Crete. People from all parts of the two islands sought medicine from her. Aliki spent whole days gathering herbs on Tripiti. And then when that black cat turned up, the one that was always with her, people believed that it took Kiki's place, some even thought it was Kiki herself.

Igor suddenly stood and said he had to go. It was night. This was the time Igor usually returned, it wasn't clear to me where he would be going. As he went out, he told me not to leave, if anyone knocked on the door, I shouldn't open it, the islanders were furious at Aliki's death. They connected her death with us.

A SLAP: PENELOPE

The small procession moved slowly from Aliki's house to the graveyard. When I joined them, they were already at the church. Ah, you don't even know. Aliki, the herbalist, is dead. This morning the priest came to our house once again, this time he didn't come inside. When I opened the door, he didn't even want to chat with me. He told Mihalis he had something serious he needed to discuss with him, and he dragged him off almost as far as the Russians' house. When Mihalis came back, he looked at me reproachfully and said nothing. His silence has always frightened me. Even when he set off towards Aliki's house he didn't call for me to come, then when I approached the procession he acted as though he didn't see me. Kiki didn't come to the burial, she remained shut in her room, looking in the distance and repeating from time to time, 'After all, she went first.' That reminded me of your first attempt at escape.

The day that Sister Makrina died, you tried to go out the gate of the convent. Sister Xanthe saw you lagging behind the procession and she suspected that you were planning something. When she saw you head slowly towards the gate, she told Olympia to make you turn back. You were nearly there when Olympia stepped out in front of you. You just smiled at her and told her you wanted to gather flowers for Sister Makrina, but you turned back. After the burial, while we were sitting under the olive tree, you swore to me that you didn't want to run away, that if you decided to escape, you would take me with you, that you just wanted to avoid being at the burial. I believed you then. I hadn't wanted to be at the burial either.

I didn't even know Sister Makrina; when I came to the convent she was already old and was also shut in her room. One afternoon you told me that you had been to her room, and that even though she was ninety years old, Sister Makrina spoke about herself as if she were a young girl. That same afternoon you took me to her room, she was sitting on the bed. When she saw us, she told us to play with dolls and the two of us burst out laughing. We were laughing so loud that Sister Theoktisti heard us and came in. That was the first time in my life that I was slapped.

And today after Aliki's burial I received my second slap.

When we returned to the house, just as I closed the door behind me, Mihalis hit me, he told me that the priest had told him that Spiros had seen me and the Russian woman at Aliki's. That Aliki's death was connected with the Russians. Then he said that they were going to gather in the church and decide what to do with them, and that they would likely also be talking about me.

* * *

He returned home late at night. He sat at the table with the bottle of raki in front of him. I stood and waited for him to pronounce the punishment. Deep inside I wanted him to say that I, along with the Russians, would have to leave the island, for a moment a small spark of hope appeared that I might leave after all. Without looking into my eyes, he said to me, 'You are never going anywhere. You will stay here forever.'

AN UNEXPECTED VISITOR: OKSANA

Igor finally appeared the following day. There was a young woman with him, about thirty years old. She stood shyly behind him. Igor said something to her in Greek, and she greeted me in Russian. Her name is Zoe, she is a teacher on the island. That is all Igor said, then he said he would make us all something to eat. The two of us were left alone. From time to time we would look at each other and smile. Igor was in an unusually good mood. He said that from now on they would sleep in the room upstairs and I would sleep in his bed. Zoe loved the sea. 'She will definitely like that room,' he said. I felt a bit of envy towards the girl. I knew nothing about her. Igor said he would try to find someone to take us to Crete and that we would leave the island as soon as possible. When he went out, Zoe retired to the room upstairs. It wasn't till evening, when Igor returned, that she came down.

During dinner, which Zoe prepared this time, the two of them sat opposite each other. He kept winking at her and she would laugh shyly. I felt like a third wheel at the table. When I tried to leave the table without them noticing, Zoe turned to me and told me that she spoke Russian, she had learned it at school, she thought she had forgotten it but when Igor appeared, what she remembered of the language came back to her. Here she looked at him again and he winked at her and she smiled at him. Igor wiped his mouth and hands with the white cloth napkin with two olives embroidered along the edge, he sat up straight and adopted a serious tone. 'Neither you nor Zoe is safe, so we decided that instead of being in two houses we'd be in one, that will be best. That way both of you will feel safer. When they discovered that

Zoe and I were seeing each other, they stopped sending the child to school.' This time Zoe was silent and looked at the fish bones on her plate. After a pause, Igor continued in the same serious tone: 'Today, after the burial, the priest gathered all the men in church. That's where they felt the safest. They couldn't talk in the taverna on account of Katerina, they're afraid of the women, they don't trust them, they think they might betray them. As far as I could figure out, Spiros will be charged with following me, you and Zoe must remain indoors at all times. Every few hours, one of them will go down to the harbour in Karave, so if we get away, they'll know. They'll leave us alone, they'll give us room to escape, we have one week, if in a week we don't get ourselves out alive, they are ready to send us off...' Here he stopped talking, he didn't want to say the word that frightened Zoe. It was all the same to me. 'How do you know all this?' I asked to break the unpleasant silence. Zoe, who most likely hadn't thought of this before, raised her head and looked at him with curiosity, in her look I could even see a small dose of disbelief. 'I have my informant. He'll arrange a boat for our departure. As soon as we leave the harbour in Karave, I'll tell you who I'm talking about.'

Following our after-dinner conversation, Igor came to my room. I was already lying down, he moved aside the blanket and sat beside me. 'You're probably wondering how I met Zoe.' I didn't answer, I waited for him to continue speaking. 'That evening when I didn't come home, when it was raining hard, I didn't spend that evening in the stable like I told you, I went to her place. That evening I knocked on her door because I knew she'd let me in, she's also a foreigner here. First a friendship developed between Zoe and me, and then a relationship.' As he was leaving, he turned and said, 'After Evgenii's death I was worried about you. You were so lonely, you talked to yourself all the time.'

I wanted to talk about you, but I haven't mentioned you to anyone, not even to Evgenii. Whenever I wanted to tell someone about you, about your father who was a cartographer and who loved most of all drawing maps of islands, about your unexpected departure, I had the sense that I would lose you forever, that even your memory would fade like the postcard your father brought you and of which I dreamed.

Maybe when we get in the boat, I will tell everything to him and Zoe.

FIRE: PENELOPE

Since that day, Mihalis stopped speaking to me. If he wanted to tell me something, he passed it on through Irini. That made me firmer in my decision to drink all the herbs. When I looked for the paper packet in which the herbs were wrapped, I saw that it wasn't under my pillow. I began to search the whole bed, then around the room. It wasn't anywhere. I was sure that Mihalis had found it and taken it. When I went into the kitchen to tell him to give it back to me, that he had to give it back to me, I was prepared to tell him everything, that I didn't want this child, that I hadn't wanted to give birth to Irini either, that I had never loved him, that I wanted to vomit from his smell of sheep and sweat, that I hated him and the island, but he wasn't there. The kitchen was empty. I sat on the chair by the window trying to think where it could be. The pillow was still there with the embroidery needle still stuck into the unfinished oar. I had begun to search around the kitchen when Irini came in, on her lips that evil smile, the one she always had when she was going to do something naughty, her hands behind her back. First she took out one hand and waved it in the air several times, showing that it was empty, then she showed the second hand, in her palm she held the crumpled packet of herbs. 'Is this what you're looking for?' she asked and threw it in the fire in the stove.

I watched as my only hope for escape burned.

If you hadn't fled that evening from the convent, we would now be somewhere in Portugal or Spain. That morning after you escaped, I woke and saw that your bed was empty. I went to our tree, but you weren't there either. When I returned, I saw Sister Erotea and Olympia searching the convent. When they saw me, Olympia told me to follow her, Sister Theoktisti was waiting for me. First she shouted at me, then she tried nicely to find out where you had gone, then she yelled at me again, even after she was certain I knew nothing, she told me I could go, but if I thought of anything, I should tell her. I was angry that you had gone like that without even saying goodbye, without even telling me where you were going and whether you were coming back for me. We were supposed to escape together. Every day, right at noon, I would go to the tree and wait for you, I thought you would show up and take me with you. One morning while I was making my bed a small piece of paper fell from under the pillow, on it was written: 'Today at noon, I will wait for you by the olive trees. I will be under our tree. Be careful so no one notices you and don't bring anything with you. Marina.'

That was the happiest morning of my life. I behaved as if everything were normal, I tried to be as inconspicuous as possible. When noon came, as soon as I was sure that everyone was in their rooms resting, I went out, but I took all my pictures with me, I couldn't leave them behind. When I got to the olive orchard, I ran towards our tree and I saw you sitting there waiting for me. I raced, thinking, 'You didn't deceive me,' my pictures were flying in all directions, I just wanted to reach you. When I got nearer the tree, I saw it wasn't you, it was Olympia, sitting there laughing. At that moment I wanted to be dead, to perish, to feel nothing. Olympia stood, grabbed me by the elbow, and dragged me off to Sister Theoktisti. She was sitting there smoking. That was the first time I saw that even nuns smoked. 'So where were you running, huh?' she said to me. 'Your friend isn't here.' She and Olympia both began to laugh.

After that day, Sister Theoktisti spread the word that there was a girl to be married off in the convent; men came from all the surrounding villages, and from Magarikari, and from Melambes and from Lagolio, there was even a doctor from Ierapetra. But Sister Theoktisti didn't give me to any of them. One day she summoned me and when I went in, I saw her sitting there with a man. 'Get ready, you're getting married,' she said. That was Mihalis. Olympia came with me to help me pack. Six months had passed since your escape. I had no news of you. While I was getting ready, Olympia told me that she regretted being so mean to me, that now, when I had to leave, she was sorry, everyone leaves and only she is always left behind. I was sorry for her, too. I wasn't angry at her. When I was all packed, she told me that Sister Theoktisti wanted to marry me off as far away as possible so you could never find me if you decided to return. She had asked the fisherman who brought fish to the convent to send word to Gavdos that on Crete, in the Convent of the Virgin Mary near Mires, there was a girl for marrying.

Irini ran from the kitchen, but I stayed to stare into the fire, I saw Crete, I saw Spain and Portugal, I saw the snow on Psiloritis, I saw El Greco, and I saw you and I saw the wicked smiles of Olympia as she told me that you had escaped and of Irini telling me I would never escape.

FIRE: OKSANA

Zoe and I were sitting at the table in the kitchen and I was helping her make lunch. Igor returned earlier than expected. It was still daytime. When he came in, I thought he would be happy when he saw Zoe and me sitting together and that I was helping her improve her language. Without even greeting us, Igor went to the room upstairs. He didn't appear for a long time. Zoe and I sat there and looked at each other in confusion. Now, with only a few days separating us from our departure, Igor had begun to act strangely. When he finally came down, he told us we were leaving that evening, not from the island, from the house. We might have to spend a few days in a cave near the beach at Sarakiniko. Zoe and I were taken aback, we didn't know what we should do, whether we were supposed to pack everything or just enough for the days until we left. I saw that he was also confused. He thought a while, then said we needed to wait until dark, and then Zoe should go to the school to get her money so we could pay the fisherman who would take us across to Crete, while we stayed here and waited for her to return; before dawn we would set off to Sarakiniko, all three of us. Kostas would try to pass on our new location to the fisherman. Kostas, so he was the informant, I thought. As if he read my mind, Igor turned to me and said, 'Well, he is also a foreigner here, he knows very well what it means to be an outcast.' 'What happened? Why did the plan suddenly change?' asked Zoe. 'Stella, the crazy woman from the lighthouse, killed herself this morning.' We were all silent. Even though I had never seen her, my eyes filled with tears. 'This morning I went earlier than usual to the lighthouse, I thought that now that all three of us are together in one place, I don't need to wait until dark to go to Zoe's, I can get back earlier and we can all eat together. When I went down to the rock, she wasn't there. I had just cast my fishing line into the water when I heard someone approaching me, I thought it was Spiros, I turned and saw that it was Stella. She was wearing a white scarf on her head. For the first time our eyes met. I thought she would say something to me, but she turned and headed towards the rock. She stood there like she always did and looked towards Crete. Suddenly, she untied the scarf and began to wave. I thought she had seen a boat, a fisherman. The sea was empty. There was no one. Stella kept waving. She had a smile on her lips. From the rock she slowly lowered herself into the sea. The water came up to her waist. Stella kept on waving. I called to her to go back, there was no one there. She kept waving and walking in deeper and deeper. I didn't know what to do, whether I should jump in after her and pull her out. In a moment she was gone, only the white scarf was above the water, and she was waving it. When she was completely gone, I ran towards the rock to jump into the water, but then out of nowhere Spiros darted in and stopped me, giving me a sign to leave her. Later he told the others that Stella and I had been talking about something, and that's why Stella, in tears, had jumped into the sea, while I just sat there and watched her drown. That completely enraged everyone, and they jumped up and wanted to run straight to the house, but Kostas stopped them, he told them to wait and consider what would be best.' Igor fell silent, we were also silent. I had wanted so much to go with him to the lighthouse and see the crazy woman standing on the rock. To break the silence, Zoe asked whether she could leave for the school. Igor told her to wait a little. 'Stella was born in Chania, on Crete. She came from a poor family. She was the second of seven children. Two boys and five girls. Her father died of tuberculosis after the seventh child was born. Her mother was a seamstress. She sewed day and night so she could feed her children. Stella was the oldest girl, she tended the house, and when she had free time, she sewed with her mother. Several months before Stella turned sixteen, her mother sewed her a dress from leftover material for her birthday. Stella waited impatiently for the day she could put on the new dress and go to a party. All her friends always went to parties, but Stella had to stay home and help her mother. That first of June 1971, Stella got up before everyone, put the house in order, washed up, and put on the new dress. With impatience she waited for 6 o'clock to arrive so she could go to the party. It was to be the first party of her life. The whole week before she had thought about how she danced and about how all the men from the neighbouring villages and from Chania would look only at her. Now, now after she turned sixteen, nothing could get in her way, the whole world was hers. Stella's happiness didn't last long. Before her friends arrived to collect her for the party, Katina, her father's sister, came over and had brought a young man with her. Katina introduced him as a student and a future captain of a ship. Stella sat in the courtyard and waited for her mother to allow her to go inside. A short time later one of her sisters came out and told her to go in. The sister left and the only ones still inside were her mother, her aunt, and the young man. Katina pushed her mother to begin talking. "From now on, parties are over for you," her mother told her. "Change your clothes. You aren't going anywhere. This is Giorgos, your fiancé." Stella flew out of the room and hid behind the house where she always hid when she wanted to be alone, and she cried for all the parties that had never begun but were over already, for all the male glances that would never gaze at her. Giorgos had come from Gavdos to finish high school in Chania and then to enrol in the university. Katina, who was a widow, rented part of her house to students, and when they finished their schooling, she found opportunities for them to marry. But Giorgos never finished university, instead of becoming captain of a ship and provider of the rich life for Stella and her family that had been promised, he became a lighthouse keeper on Gavdos. Instead of the life full of parties she had imagined, her days were interminable, no one came to the house by the lighthouse. For days on end the silence was killing her, and when she would go out to walk, all the craggy rocks and stones on the island seemed like ghosts, and wherever she went, they appeared in front of her. The quiet was so intense that she was afraid to open her mouth; occasionally she would let out a deep cry that no one heard. She dragged herself to the room that looked out on the sea, towards freedom, where there were no rocky cliffs and stones. Over the course of time she began to forget the days, the months, she was forgetting everything.'

Zoe stood and said it was time to go. As she was leaving, before she closed the door, she waved to us as if she were bidding us farewell. I wanted to take something from the island as well. I remembered the stone that Igor had given me, the stone from the crazy woman. After a long time, I went again to the upstairs room. The stone was lying where I had left it, on the windowsill. My gaze passed across the empty bed, for a moment I felt nostalgia for all those days spent in this room, those days when Evgenii was still coherent.

* * *

As I was heading down the wooden stairs from the upper floor, I heard breaking glass. I shouted to Igor but there was no answer. In the house was dead silence. I stood between the two floors, stuck on the stairs, waiting to see what would happen. I heard glass breaking, this time in the distance. After a few minutes I went down a few more steps, but before I reached the lower floor I heard Igor shouting at me to go back up. As I ran to the room on the upper floor, I heard more glass break behind me. I sat in the room and waited for Igor to come. Most likely someone had betrayed us and now the enraged people had gathered in front of our house. But why wasn't Igor coming? Where was Igor? Now I don't even hear the sound of breaking glass. I head towards the lower floor, I go down the stairs, and I see the house is burning. The fire prevents me from going down. Igooooooor, Igooooooor I shout, but no one answers me. The fire is already near the stairs, it will soon devour the upstairs room. Igor, where is Igor? Has Zoe come back? Zoeeeee… I call, but no one calls back. Now the wooden stairs are beginning to burn. I climb up to the room, but the smoke follows me. My chest is filled with smoke. With it comes our teacher, Ruslana Anatolievna Bondar. Her hair is gathered in a braid. Her eyebrows are joined, there are two deep furrows on her forehead. Whenever she wanted to say something serious, she knitted her eyebrows. She pulls out a handkerchief from the sleeve of her blouse, she blows her nose, and returns the handkerchief to her sleeve. She needs time to say what she wants to say. Everyone is looking at her in anticipation, I am the only one looking at the empty seat where you sat. She breathes deeply and begins to speak. Her tone is formal. She says something I don't quite understand, but I know that after that, your turn will come. Finally, I hear your father's name, and then yours. He was sitting in his study drawing a new map of an island. You were sleeping in the next room with your mother. He fell asleep with a cigarette in his hand. First to catch fire was the paper on which he was drawing, then another, a third… The whole house burned with you inside it. Before me I saw thousands of islands in flame. I saw the trees aflame with their olives, oranges, oleander, bougainvillea, the stone houses… I couldn't imagine you then, but now I see you in flames as you stand in the midst of fire, you are still a young girl, you will always be a young girl. I want to shout aloud, I want to shout for you, to shout for myself, but instead of my voice, what emerges is black smoke. I look towards the door, but Igor is not there, only the fire that draws closer to me. I want to shout, but I cannot.

I want to ask, where is Igor?
Did Igor exist?
Did you exist?
Evgenii?
The island?

I try to push out at least a small sound of my voice. There are so many things I want to ask. I want to shout for Zoe, too. Did Zoe exist? I shout, but in vain. I want to ask, did I exist? But who, who is there to tell me?

Some of the characters are real, the stories about them and some historical events have been invented in the interests of the story.

The poems 'Marina of the Rocks' by Odysseus Elytis and 'Walls' by Constantine P. Cavafy are cited in the novel.

PARTHIAN TRANSLATIONS

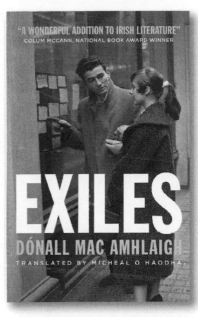

EXILES

Dónall Mac Amhlaigh

Translated from Irish
by Mícheál Ó hAodha

Out October 2020

£12.00
978-1-912681-31-0

HANA

Alena Mornštajnová

Translated from Czech
by Julia and Peter Sherwood

Out October 2020

£10.99
978-1-912681-50-1

Creative
Europe

LA BLANCHE
Maï-Do Hamisultane

Translated from French
by Suzy Ceulan Hughes

£8.99
978-1-912681-23-5

THE NIGHT CIRCUS
AND OTHER STORIES
Uršuľa Kovalyk

Translated from Slovak
by Julia and Peter Sherwood

£8.99
978-1-912681-04-4

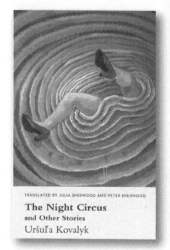

A GLASS EYE
Miren Agur Meabe

Translated from Basque
by Amaia Gabantxo

£8.99
978-1-912109-54-8

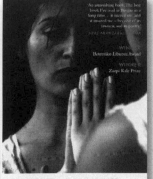

Creative
Europe

PARTHIAN TRANSLATIONS

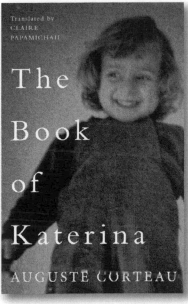

THE BOOK OF KATERINA

Auguste Corteau

Translated from Greek by Claire Papamichail

Out 2021

£10.00
978-1-912681-26-6

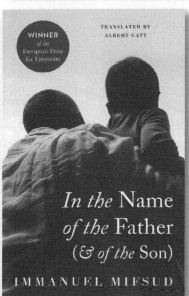

IN THE NAME OF THE FATHER (& OF THE SON)

Immanuel Mifsud

Translated from Maltese by Albert Gatt

£6.99
978-1-912681-30-3

Creative Europe

HER MOTHER'S HANDS

Karmele Jaio

Translated from Basque
by Kristin Addis

£8.99
978-1-912109-55-5

WOMEN WHO
BLOW ON KNOTS

Ece Temelkuran

Translated from Turkish
by Alexander Dawe

£9.99
978-1-910901-69-4

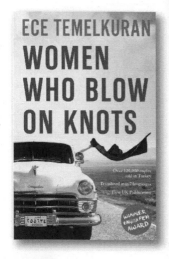

THE HOUSE OF
THE DEAF MAN

Peter Krištúfek

Translated from Slovak
by Julia and Peter Sherwood

£11.99
978-1-909844-27-8

PARTHIAN TRANSLATIONS

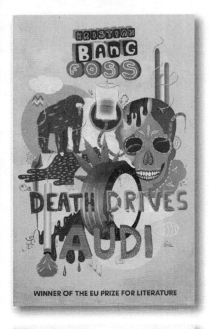

DEATH DRIVES AN AUDI

Kristian Bang Foss

Winner of the European Prize for Literature

£10.00
978-1-912681-32-7

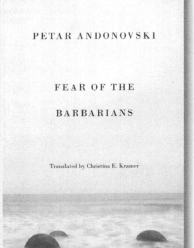

FEAR OF BARBARIANS

Petar Adonovski

Winner of the European Prize for Literature

£9.00
978-1-913640-19-4

Creative Europe

PARTHIAN TRANSLATIONS

FLOWERS OF WAR

Llyr Gwyn Lewis

Short-Listed for Wales
Book of the Year

£9.00
978-1-912681-25-9

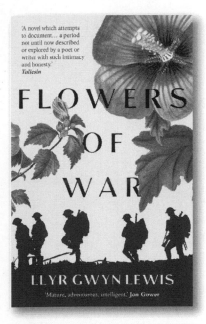

'A novel which attempts
to document... a period
not until now described
or explored by a poet or
writer with such intimacy
and honesty.'
Taliesin

FLOWERS
OF
WAR

LLYR GWYN LEWIS

'Mature, adventurous, intelligent.' **Jon Gower**

MARTHA, JACK AND SHANCO

Caryl Lewis

Winner of the Wales
Book of the Year

Out October 2020

£9.99
978-1-912681-77-8

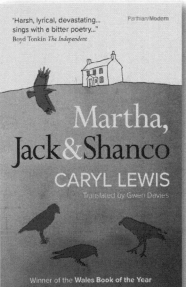

'Harsh, lyrical, devastating...
sings with a bitter poetry..."
Boyd Tonkin *The Independent*

Parthian/Modern

Martha,
Jack & Shanco

CARYL LEWIS
Translated by Gwen Davies

Winner of the **Wales Book** of the Year

Creative
Europe